THE AMAZING SPIDER-MAN 2

Adapted by BRITTANY CANDAU AND NACHIE MARSHAM

Based on the screenplay by ALEX KURTZMAN &
ROBERTO ORCI & JEFF PINKNER

Produced by AVI ARAD & MATT TOLMACH

Directed by MARC WEBB

NEW YORK • LOS ANGELES

MARVEL © MARVEL marvelkids.com © 2014 CPII

All rights reserved. Published by Marvel Press, an imprint of
Disney Book Group. No part of this book may be reproduced
or transmitted in any form or by any means, electronic or
mechanical, including photocopying, recording, or by any
information storage and retrieval system, without written
permission from the publisher. For information, address
Marvel Press, 1101 Flower Street, Glendale, California 91201.

Printed in the United States of America

First Edition

1 3 5 7 9 10 8 6 4 2

V475-2873-0-14046

ISBN 978-1-4231-9758-4

SUSTAINABLE
FORESTRY
INITIATIVE

Certified Chain of Custody
Promoting Sustainable Forestry

www.sfiprogram.org
SFI-01054
The SFI label applies to the text stock

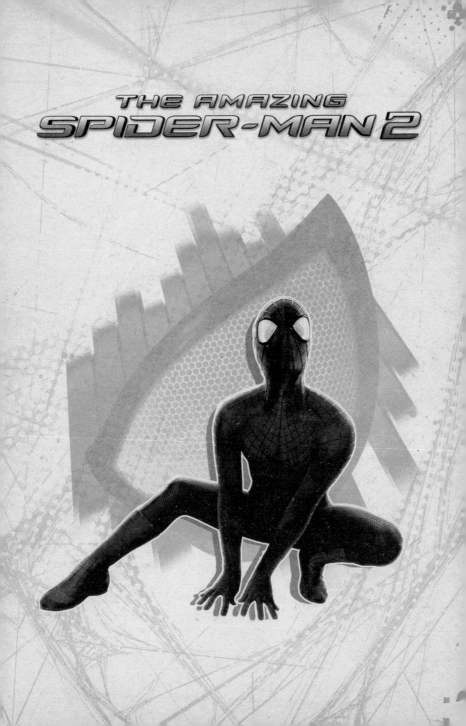

CHAPTER 1

IN WHICH SPIDER-MAN FINDS SOME PLUTONIUM BUT LOSES HIS SHOES

THE TIRES of the tow truck screeched loudly as it made a tight turn and accelerated down the street. It wasn't the first time a tow truck had driven way too fast down the streets of Manhattan. It probably wasn't even the first time a tow truck hauling an Oscorp armored car had gone shooting down the streets of Midtown. However, it probably *was* the first time a tow truck driven by a tattooed mobster had sped down a street in Midtown Manhattan while towing a stolen Oscorp truck full of plutonium.

Probably.

"Get out of my way!" the driver of the truck yelled

1

while swerving through the streets. The police were chasing him, but Aleksei, the tattooed man behind the wheel, wasn't alone. His fellow thieves were armed and ready to hold off the police as they made their getaway.

As the truck neared Times Square, a colorful cross section of humanity stood on the sidewalks, watching the high-speed chase get closer and closer. Tourists, construction workers, office drones, and people dressed in lively costumes passing out advertisements stood shoulder to shoulder, craning their necks to get a better look at the action. A guy dressed like Spider-Man leaned over to a woman dressed like the Statue of Liberty. "Hey, there," said the guy in the Spider-Man costume. "What's happening?"

"An Oscorp truck was on a delivery run, some guys hijacked it," said the woman in the Statue of Liberty outfit, looking over the quality of the Spidey suit. "*Nice* outfit."

"Thanks," said Spidey. "You, too."

The sirens were getting closer as the Statue of Liberty continued. "Anyway, they've been going for, like, seventy-four blocks. They say it's carrying plutonium—you know, radioactive! Man, if one of those canisters blows . . ." She trailed off as the tow truck shot by them.

"You had me at 'plutonium,'" said the guy in the Spidey suit, leaning dangerously off the sidewalk and into the street. As the police cars shot by, he reached out and grabbed one of them. He was pulled off his feet, sticking to the side of the car. The Statue of Liberty could only look, shocked, as the car chase disappeared down the street. That was not a costume! She'd been talking to the real Spider-Man!

Spidey hadn't been planning on getting involved. He had places to go and people to see, and he knew better than most how good the police were at catching criminals. But as soon as he heard about the radioactive materials rocketing through the streets of New York, he knew what needed to be done. He jumped from the police car, flew into the air, and fired a strand of webbing toward the cop car in front of him, quickly moving up the stream of cars that were chasing the tow truck.

As he jumped into the air, aiming for the police car directly behind the speeding truck full of angry mobsters, the front page of the newest edition of *The Daily Bugle* fluttered up and plastered itself to his face. Dropping onto the hood of a police car, he leaped off, corkscrewed in the air, and landed on the truck while looking at the newspaper. It was a giant picture of his head with a headline that read SPIDER-MENACE in large letters. "That's not even clever!" Spider-Man said, tossing the paper into the air and returning to the matter at hand.

He swung to the driver's side of the truck, seemingly oblivious to the chaos all around him. "Hi!" he cheerily said to the truck's driver. "I'm Spider-Man. Not my given name, obviously . . ."

The driver frantically swerved the truck back and forth to shake Spider-Man loose. It wasn't going to help, seeing as how the hero's spider-like abilities let him stick to the truck like glue.

He didn't even need to use both hands, which was made clear when he reached out to the driver and tried to shake his hand. The driver, equal parts enraged and annoyed, shouted in a deep Russian accent at the top of his lungs, "GET OFF!"

"So you're not a shaker?" asked Spider-Man. "Are you a hugger? Look, not to rush you, but I'm running a little late. Can we just cut to the part where you start to cry and give up?"

He looked ahead of the speeding truck, trying to find a good spot to bring it to a halt. But before he could do anything, the driver barked an order in Russian into a walkie-talkie.

"What *is* that accent?" Spider-Man asked. "Boston? Philly?" He craned his neck to see who the driver was talking to and noticed that the back of the armored car the truck was towing had opened. Before he knew it, a metal container was flying out! The driver must have told his partners in crime to toss one of the several containers of plutonium to distract Spider-Man. The wall-crawler instantly did a backflip off the front of the truck, twisted in midair, and shot a stream of webbing at a container that was rolling on the street.

He pulled the container to himself and swung to the roof of a nearby police car. He knew he had to catch up to the truck and stop the criminals from getting away, but he had to leave the dangerous substance somewhere safe first. "Do NOT drop this!" he said to the police officer in the car. "TWO HANDS!" The startled cop took the container from Spider-Man and watched as the red-and-blue hero jumped back into action, swinging at high speed after the truck dragging the stolen armored car.

Nearby, a man named Max Dillon hurried down the crowded sidewalk. He was wearing a blue jumpsuit with his Oscorp employee badge attached to the pocket of his shirt. Carrying an armful of blueprints, he had the look of someone constantly distracted from what was in front of him. Max was trying to get to work, but the street was jammed full of people who kept bumping into him. "Excuse me," Max uttered to a man in a suit. "Excuse me," he said again, after being jostled by another person. "Hey—ow!—hey, *person here . . .*" Another busy commuter bumped into Max's arms, knocking one of his blueprints loose.

"Hey!" Max exclaimed, reaching down into the street to grab his blueprint before it could roll away.

He had been so focused on trying to get to work he hadn't heard the sirens from the police who were chasing the fleeing truck, or the truck roaring down the street. He looked up, just in time to see the truck hit a parked taxi with a massive *KRUNCH!* The taxi went flying, straight at Max!

Fortunately, Spider-Man *had* seen all this and was able to grab Max a split second before the taxi crashed into the street where he had been standing. "You!" Max uttered, stunned. "You—you're Spider-Man!"

"Costume totally gave me away, huh, Max?" said Spider-Man.

"You . . . do you know me?" Max asked, confused. He was a low-level electrical engineer for Oscorp. He had always felt like no one knew his name.

"Your badge," Spider-Man said, pointing at the Oscorp ID pinned to Max's shirt pocket. He pointed to the blueprints Max was clutching in his arms. "Those look important." Spidey and Max landed. Max tried to answer, but was starstruck. This was his hero, Spider-Man!

"They—they are. They're building a new power

grid, and I have some ideas—I mean, some thoughts, some notions," he rattled off quickly, clearly excited about the chance to prove himself. "People treat me like I'm nobody, but I'm gonna show 'em I'm somebody—"

"No, no. You *are* somebody, Max," Spider-Man said. "You're my eyes and ears out there. I need you, okay? Stay safe!" And just like that, he was gone—leaping into the air, and swinging after the escaping truck and its stolen cargo.

"Okay!" said Max, inspired by Spider-Man's heroism. "Then that's what I am: your eyes and ears. Wow . . . Spider-Man!"

Spider-Man had just about caught up to the damaged truck when he saw that the police had set up a roadblock ahead. The truck sped up. They were going to ram the barricade! The police clearly had their hands full. The criminals climbed to the back of the Oscorp truck and began tossing some of the radioactive containers onto the street while two more goons leaned out with weapons ready to fire!

Before they could open fire, Spider-Man webbed

the guns out of their hands. He quickly threw himself into the back of the truck, using his speed and his strength to knock out the thugs. Just then, the driver floored it, shooting the truck forward even faster! The remaining containers holding the plutonium had been knocked loose in the struggle, and some of them started to fly out of the truck as it picked up speed.

Spider-Man saw that six containers were falling out of the truck and toward the street, where they'd be run over by the police cars chasing the stolen truck! He quickly webbed the containers—one . . . two . . . three . . . four . . . five . . . all safe and stuck to the insides of the truck. But the last one hit the ground, the edge of the containment canister breaking! The tube holding the dangerous plutonium rolled out, and Spider-Man launched himself from the speeding truck to catch it. He was able to grab the tube, but a SWAT van was bearing down on him with no time to stop!

Somehow, Spider-Man was able to grab the front of the van. There he was, holding on to both the van and a tube containing a dangerous substance, when his phone went off, and there was only one person it could be. . . .

"Hi, I'm on my way," Spider-Man said, trying to sound as casual as possible. "Got stuck in traffic."

"Your timing's terrible. It *started*," said Gwen Stacy, standing in front of a bright blue-and-yellow banner reading "Congratulations. Midtown Science High School Graduates." She was wearing a blue-and-yellow cap and gown—and, as usual, she was a little bit worried about Peter Parker. Over the phone, she could hear the faint sound of sirens and the not-so-faint sound of air rushing by at high speeds. "Where are you right now?" she said into the phone, afraid to hear the answer.

"Umm . . . the corner of First and Broadway," said Peter. "Wait, Second and Broadway," he said a moment later, with what sounded like even more sirens in the background. "Third and Broadway—I'll be there! Five minutes."

"What's happening?" Gwen said quietly into her phone. "Are those sirens? Peter? Are you there?"

Just then, while holding on to the front of the

SWAT van zooming down the street, Spider-Man saw something that made his blood run cold. Time seemed to stand still.

Sitting in one of the police cars rushing by, staring straight into Spider-Man's eyes, was Gwen's father: Captain George Stacy.

Except Peter knew that was impossible. Captain Stacy had died more than a year ago protecting Spider-Man from the rampaging creature called the Lizard. And as he lay dying, he made Peter promise to break things off with Gwen. Captain Stacy knew that Peter's secret life as Spider-Man would endanger the people closest to him. So Peter had promised the dying man he'd follow his wishes. But ultimately, that was a promise he could not keep. He cared for Gwen, deeply, and he knew she felt the same way about him. She knew about his life as Spider-Man; he trusted her completely. But no matter how much he told himself things would be okay, he also knew he had broken his promise to Captain Stacy—that there were some things even Spider-Man couldn't do—and he was terrified he would put the lives of his loved ones in danger.

"Uh, I gotta go," said Spider-Man softly. "There's someone on the other line." And with that, he hung up.

Gwen was more or less used to this by now. She and Peter had been together long enough for her to know he had his issues and crises to handle, and she had hers. And it was just about time for her to handle her own challenge.

She swallowed her concerns for Peter and walked onto the graduation stage to deliver her valedictory address. Looking out at the hundreds of people, she said, "Esteemed faculty, family, friends, and fellow graduates, I'd like to start with a question I know everyone here's wondering, but no one's willing to ask: is Principal Conway *actually* naked under his gown?"

The gathering of students, teachers, and families all laughed with her. She just hoped Peter was going to be able to handle whatever was going on at his end of the phone.

Five to ten minutes away from the Midtown High graduation ceremony, Spider-Man looked up and realized the SWAT van was getting closer and closer to the stolen truck. When he looked back at one of the pursuing police cars, Gwen's father appeared again to be sitting in one. But his mind was playing tricks on him.

Holding on to the tube of plutonium tightly, he quickly jumped from the SWAT van back to the front of the tow truck. The tattooed driver, who had thought he had seen the last of Spider-Man, looked even more furious than before. Screaming in Russian, he twisted the steering wheel hard, ramming the truck into a bus!

The good news was that the truck finally came to a sudden, loud, incredibly jarring halt filled with broken glass and what Spider-Man could only assume were Russian curse words. The bad news was that the bus had been hit so hard it was sliding toward more pedestrians!

Spider-Man tossed the plutonium tube toward a street post, webbing it into place, and dove in front of the bus! Thanks to him, the vehicle came to a halt ahead of the sidewalk. There was only one thing left for him to do, and that was to catch the guy who had started the mad chase in the first place. Fortunately, he was the only enraged Russian in a tracksuit carrying a submachine gun and a tube of plutonium on the street that day, so he wasn't hard to find.

Spider-Man jumped into action before the guy could shoot into the crowded street, grabbing the gun with a quickly fired blast of webbing. Before the tattooed man knew it, he had been stripped of his firearm and the last stolen tube of plutonium, had his arms and legs webbed into place to keep him still, and—for good measure—had his pants yanked down by an extra blast of webbing. His mouth, however, was still working just fine.

"This is not the end, Spider!" he screamed, veins bulging. "I vill crush you!"

"I got it!" said Spider-Man. "Your accent . . . it's Russian?"

Spider-Man handed the dangerous plutonium off to one of the policemen who were swarming around the scene now that the truck had been stopped, then jumped back into the air. It was a job well done, but his day was just getting started.

Gwen's valedictory speech was ending as Peter

tried to sneak unnoticed into the ceremony. "I know we all think we're immortal. We're supposed to feel that way—we're graduating. Our future is and should be bright. But like our brief four years in high school, what makes life valuable is that it doesn't last forever. What makes it precious is that it ends. I know that now more than ever.

"And I say it, today of all days, to remind us that time . . . is luck. So don't waste it living someone else's life. Make yours count for something. Fight for what matters to you. No matter what. Even if we fall short, what better way is there to live?"

After the applause died down, Peter joined his classmates in the line to walk across the stage and get his diploma. And as he stood up, something about him caught Gwen's eye. Not any of the things that normally caught her eye—this was a quick flash of red and blue. That was the exact moment Gwen realized Peter had changed out of his Spider-Man outfit so quickly he hadn't remembered to take off his Spidey footwear. Fortunately, she was able to get his attention. Peter ducked away unnoticed, put his sneakers on, and was able to walk across the stage in front of Gwen, his Aunt May, and everyone present.

Later, Peter and Aunt May met up in the crowd of the Midtown High graduation.

"Sorry I was late, Aunt May," Peter said to his exasperated aunt. "Traffic was a total nightmare."

"*Honestly*, Peter," May said. "I was about to steal a cap and gown and run up there myself."

"That would've made a great graduation photo," said Peter to his smiling aunt. He knew how hard she'd worked to help make sure he'd be able to stand there in his cap and gown.

"You really did it, kiddo. I'm so proud of you," she said, gazing at him. "I know what your uncle would say. . . ."

"'Party's over. Get a job,'" joked Peter.

"He'd say, 'Don't follow the path, make your own trail,'" May said to her nephew.

"Ralph W. Emerson . . ."

"See, you *did* learn something," said May. "I wish he could've been here."

"And my folks, too . . ." said Peter. From the disappearance of his parents when he was a little boy to the loss of his Uncle Ben right after he got his spider-powers, Peter had faced tragedy his entire life. But he had been dealing with it, and May was a large part of how and why he'd been able to do so.

May saw Gwen heading toward her and Peter, and decided to give the two of them a minute alone. Gwen walked up to Peter, looking at a news story on her phone.

"Out of curiosity," she said quietly, "did your 'traffic jam' involve dodging machine-gun fire and the Russian mob?"

"Only a little?" Peter responded sheepishly.

"Why didn't you tell me?"

"I didn't want you to worry," Peter said. But before they could talk any more, they were joined by Flash Thompson, who looked as excited as Peter and Gwen had ever seen him.

"Gwendolyn!" Flash said happily, high-fiving Gwen. "I got into Dakota State! Your tutoring *totally* worked!"

"Flashua! You're damn right it did," said Gwen. "But you are aware that cows outnumber students, like, four to one out there, right?"

"Hey, four to one, that's a fraction!"

"Ratio," Gwen said to Flash. "But *so* close!" Flash wasn't the brightest in school, but he was a good friend to Peter and Gwen.

Peter looked around him. The whole area was crowded with people who were filled with joy and excitement about the future. And then he saw him again—Captain Stacy, looking exactly the way he had the night he'd died. Staring straight into Peter's eyes. Just like Peter wished his parents and Uncle Ben could have been there to see him graduate from high school, he knew Gwen would have given anything to have her father there for real. Peter stared at his feet, unable to move.

Later that night, Peter went to meet Gwen and the rest of her family for dinner in Chinatown. As he walked from the subway to the restaurant, he couldn't shake the memory of Captain Stacy.

When he got to the restaurant, Peter could see

Gwen and the Stacys inside, eating and laughing, but he couldn't bear to open the door and go inside.

"What're you doing?" he said to his reflection. "What're you doing . . . what're you doing . . . what're you doing . . ."

"Yeah, I was wondering that, too," said Gwen. She'd spotted him and come outside. "It's my father, isn't it?"

"I *see* him. Everywhere I go. I can't get him outta my head," Peter said with a faraway look in his eyes. "I made him a promise, Gwen."

"Haven't we had this conversation? It's not his choice," said Gwen. She knew Peter was worried about what could happen, but she also knew the decision about whether they stayed together was one that should belong solely to *them*. Yet she could see it was eating Peter up.

"I looked him in the eye," said Peter. "I looked him in the eye when he was dying and told him I'd stay away from you. And here I am. At dinner. With your whole family." He looked up at her. "So what does that make me?"

"I don't know, Peter," Gwen said. "What *does* that make you?"

"A liar? A phony?"

"Funny, I thought it meant you loved me."

Peter stared at Gwen. "I do. . . ."

"Well, then why isn't that enough?"

"Because what if he was *right*?" said Peter. "What if you get hurt . . . because of me? Like *he* did." He looked down at his feet again. "I can't let that happen. I can't."

Gwen forced Peter to look at her again. "Lemme tell you something about my dad, okay? He wasn't an easy man to live with—ask my mom. But she loved him, and she never asked him to be something he wasn't. You're Spider-Man. And I love that. But I love Peter Parker *more*. And that's worth it to me."

Peter couldn't shake the fear that was sitting inside him. "I can't . . . I can't lose you, too."

Gwen looked at him sharply. "Because you can't lose me, we can't be together? So who does that work out for?"

"I'm so sorry, Gwen . . ." Peter said.

Gwen couldn't believe what was happening. "You've done this to me again," she said. "And again. I can't do it anymore. I can't live like this. Now it's me: I break up with you. I break up with you. I break up with you."

She turned around and went back into the restaurant, ignoring the questioning look from her mother. By the time she sat back in her seat and looked up at the window, Peter was gone.

CHAPTER 2
WHAT A DIFFERENCE A YEAR MAKES?

ONE YEAR AFTER his high-school graduation, a lot had changed for Spider-Man. Well, some things had changed. But the situation in front of him wasn't one of them. He was swinging through New York City, keeping an eye out for anything that might need his attention, but also keeping an eye out for Gwen Stacy. It had been some time since they'd broken up, but he still hadn't been able to get her out of his head.

He saw her on the street far below. But as happy as he was to see her again, he still couldn't face her. Not yet. Before he could think about it too much, he heard sirens in the distance and saw the faint glow of a fire farther off.

It was time for Spider-Man to do his thing; he jumped headfirst from the building, swinging back into the night sky.

Peter woke up to a loud banging. He shot upright and quickly took in his surroundings. He was in his room, lying on top of his bed. He still smelled like smoke from the burning building from which he'd helped people escape the night before. He was still wearing most of his Spider-Man outfit. And Aunt May was opening the door.

Not the best way to start the day.

"Just a sec, Aunt May! I'm not dressed!" Peter said, scrambling up and trying to change out of his Spider-Man togs. "I am extremely naked!"

May, who had been trying to wake Peter up for a while, was getting tired of the runaround. "Your final starts at nine, and you said you'd take my car to the shop. It keeps dying. Peter, open the door."

There was no answer, just the sound of him

scrambling around, so she started to enter. Peter, still wearing some of Spidey's clothes, jumped back into bed and pulled the covers up to hide the red-and-blue costume.

Aunt May was used to Peter's eccentricities. He was . . . well, the boy was a bit weird. She stared at him. "Is everything okay?"

"Just overslept, that's all," said Peter.

"What happened to your face?" asked May, looking at the soot and grime on Peter's face. "It's filthy."

"It is?" Peter responded, pulling the blankets up to cover more of himself. "Huh."

"Are you cold? Are you sick?" May asked.

"Nope." Peter answered as calmly as possible. "I am neither of those things. Just . . . dirty. And late."

"Well . . . come downstairs," she said, walking out of Peter's room and closing the door behind her.

May knew Peter was trying to keep *something* a secret, even though she didn't know what. But she had her own secrets to worry about. Ever since her husband, Peter's Uncle Ben, had been killed, it had been harder and harder to make ends meet. She was still working as a waitress, but she'd also started taking nursing classes at the local hospital. As she stood in their kitchen, packing a lunch for Peter to take with him to his college classes, she was on the phone with her boss at the diner.

"I'm just asking you to find another waitress to cover me tonight," she said as she heard Peter coming down the stairs. "I start training rounds at the hospital. . . . I don't want Peter to know. It'll only worry him. I'll do a double on Thursday, okay? Lemme call you back," she said, hanging up the phone as Peter walked into the kitchen, carrying a laundry basket packed with dirty clothes.

"Eat!" she said, pointing toward the breakfast she'd made for him. "You're too skinny. I keep telling you that starving yourself is a very slow way to die. We have rat poison under the sink if you want something that'll work really fast."

"As always," Peter said through a mouthful of toast, "I thank you for your wisdom and guidance. Who was that on the phone?"

"Hmmm, what?" Aunt May said. It was her turn

to play coy about what really was going on. "Oh, nothing. Just ironing out my week."

"You're working double shifts now?" asked Peter. He always worried about his aunt, and he didn't want her to overextend herself.

"I miss Ben at night, honey," she explained. "It's easier not to be home, and the girls give me a laugh. Plus, it's a little extra to stuff under the mattress."

"I sold another couple photos to the *Bugle*," Peter said, standing up and pointing at a copy of the newspaper sitting on the kitchen table. "That oughtta help."

"That man really ought to be paying you a fair wage," May said, referring to Peter's boss at the paper.

"Jameson? He does," said Peter. "If it was 1961." He started unloading his clothes into the washing machine that was in the kitchen. May jumped up, trying to keep Peter from seeing her nurse uniform in the washing machine.

"No, no, no," she said quickly, trying to take the basket of clothes from him. "I'll do it."

"I have laundry to—" Peter began, not wanting

May to see the Spider-Man outfit he'd buried in the rest of his clothes.

"I've been doing your laundry since you were six."

"That's a long time. I'm in college now. It's time for me to take responsibility for my own underwear."

"And the last time you turned everything red and blue."

"I was washing my . . . flag."

"*Peter*. My house. My washing machine. My laundry."

Peter backed off from the washing machine while holding on to his clothes. He took a closer look at the front-page headline on the copy of *The Daily Bugle* on the kitchen table, which read: SPIDEY SETS BLAZE? Peter couldn't believe his eyes!

"What?" he said, pointing at the newspaper. "Are you kidding me? He rescued, like, fifteen people from a burning building!"

May looked quizzically at Peter. "You seem very . . . passionate . . . about this, Peter."

"Oh, no, you know," Peter backtracked. "I just— these are *lies*. *The Daily Bugle* keeps making him out to be some kind of villain! And I just think people should know that . . ."

"That what?" May asked him.

"That he's a good guy!" Peter exclaimed. "I think. . . . It seems."

"Mm-hmmm," said May. "If you feel so strongly about it, why don't you take pictures of him? Show the world who he really is?"

There was an awkward silence. Aunt May handed Peter a bag. "Here you go, Peter. Food. Boiled eggs, four chicken breasts, and almonds. Lots of almonds."

"Almonds?"

"Raw protein," she said, giving Peter a look. "Can't take on the world on an empty stomach."

"Thanks!" Peter said, grabbing his stuff and heading out the door. "Gotta fly! I mean, 'run.' I can't fly. Obviously."

And with that, Peter ran out the door, heading off to class, to his test, and to what was going to continue to be a really, really weird day.

CHAPTER 3
ELECTRO IS BORN!

MAX DILLON knew it was going to be a good day. He had big plans for his workday ahead of him at Oscorp. He was feeling good. And to make it even better, it was his birthday. He plugged his electric razor into the power strip. It was filled with a staggering number of electrical gadgets, but there was still room for one more, or so he thought. The lights flickered and then went out with a small *pop!*, followed by a shrill cry from the living room.

"Maaaaaaaaaaaaaaax!" his mother cried out. Max lived at home with his mother, and she was tired of him constantly blowing out the small apartment's power. He tried to explain to her that he was excited about his birthday and wanted to celebrate, but she didn't want to hear it. She never wanted to hear about the things that mattered to him, but he was still feeling pretty upbeat. Today was the day when he was finally going to confront his boss about something very, very important to him.

A year ago, on the day Max was saved by his hero, Spider-Man, he'd been taking a plan for a brand-new power facility to Oscorp. His boss, Alistair Smythe, had ignored his ideas, like he always did. But then, months later, Max was shocked to learn Oscorp was breaking ground on a power plant following his exact schematics. He had tried to get the courage time and time again to stand up to his boss, but today he was really going to do it!

That is, until he got stuck on the subway trying to get to the Oscorp offices and ended up late to work. Smythe was always mad when he got to work late. Well, Smythe was usually just mad in general.

"Dillon, you're late!" he said, glaring at Max as he stepped into the office.

"Sir, I got stuck on the train . . ." Max began, but

Smythe ignored him, as always. Max took a deep breath and started to explain his concerns about the Oscorp power plant to Smythe, but he didn't get very far.

"Don't you realize Oscorp's responsible for the entire city's energy supply?" said Smythe.

"Yessir, I submitted some designs for it, but I never heard anything. And then, sure enough, a bunch of 'em ended up being used and . . ."

"Sure you did, Dillon, and I'm Spider-Man," said Smythe, turning away from him. "Get to work!"

Max left Smythe's office dejected and headed for the elevator. Just as the doors started to close, he heard a woman's voice come from down the hall.

"Hold that! Can you hold that, please!"

Max grabbed the door before it could close, and Gwen Stacy ran into the elevator.

"Thank you," she said, smiling. "Thank you—thanks—you're a real gentleman. Most people would've just let them close."

"Well, most people usually don't notice . . . other people. Usually. Floor?"

"Sixty-three, please," said Gwen.

"I'm Max."

"Hi. I'm Gwen." She noticed that a birthday invitation was on the screen of the tablet he was holding. "Is today your birthday?" she asked.

"Oh, uh, yeah," Max said. He had actually made his own invitation and sent it out to his coworkers, but no one had responded.

"I made—I mean, they made—I mean, my friends made an invite. For a little party they're throwing. I'd . . . uh, I'd invite you, but the guest list is already closed, so . . ." He ended awkwardly. Most of the things that came out of Max's mouth ended awkwardly, but he was excited he was talking to someone who actually noticed him and who was paying attention to him, in even the slightest way.

He saw her red student-employee work badge. "So you go to Empire State?" he asked.

"Yeah," she said, pointing at his green badge. "Electrical engineering, huh?"

"I take care of a lot of the equipment around here. Meter calibration, voltage testing. I even gave them some new ideas for the power grid," he said, anger creeping into his voice. "But, you know, I don't expect a thank-you. It's okay. . . ."

"Dr. Stillwell showed us the specs," Gwen said brightly. "Hydroelectric power. So cool. That was you?"

Max couldn't believe his ears! He was talking to someone who knew of his work! "Yes, yes, that was me! Electricity's sort of a . . . passion? Life focus? When I was a kid and the power went out, I'd be all alone, in the dark, just praying it'd come back on, staring at the outlet, thinking—why 'outlet' when you plug things *in*? Why not 'inlet'? Then I thought, it's gotta be magic, right?" Max started talking faster and faster as he got more into the details of his love of electricity.

"Wrong, not magic—ions, electrons, all invisible. But *everywhere*. People never see what's right in front of them, you know? They're so busy running around, bumping into people, being rude, they don't notice all of that . . . power, just waiting to . . . come alive."

He looked at Gwen, hoping for some sort of connection or understanding. But she was looking behind him with an intense and faraway gleam in her eyes. He turned around and saw news footage of Spider-Man on the elevator's TV.

"Must be cool, huh?" said Max. "Have the world see you like that? Like on TV. He saved my life once. All the people in this city, and Spider-Man saved *me*. He said he needed me."

"Oh?" said Gwen, looking away from the TV. "That must be . . . a good feeling."

"Yeah. Nice to be needed." The elevator reached Gwen's floor, and she walked out of the car. "Nice to meet you, Max."

"You too, Gwen," Max said as the doors closed. "Hey, you remembered my name!"

Max was looking forward to heading home after another long day at Oscorp. But just then . . .

"Dillon. Got a current-flow problem in the chemical genomics lab," said Smythe, walking into Max's work area. Smythe was clearly about to leave—but as usual, Max was going to have to stay behind.

"But everyone else has already left. Why do I have to—" Max started to protest, but Smythe cut him off.

"Because you're special, Dillon. And don't expect overtime."

Max headed down to the chemical genomics lab, which was one of the areas inside the Oscorp building where scientists worked tirelessly on experimental procedures. It was a lab much like that one in which, years ago, Dr. Curtis Connors had accidentally turned himself into the monstrous creature called the Lizard. It was a lab that promised the advances in knowledge, in bioengineering, and in profits that Norman Osborn had worked hard to attain through science and technology.

But right now, it was a room full of fancy machinery and giant electric eels in a tank filled with water. A room where the power wasn't working. And that made it a room Max Dillon was needed in.

"'Max, make sure everything's working,'" Max muttered angrily to himself while taking his tools out. "'Max, fix this! Max, fix that!' All people do is order me around. *I'm* the guy who makes the city run. Those hydroelectric towers? My design. They *stole* it."

On the computer screens and video monitors throughout the lab was the AI known as Kari that kept all the computerized facilities at Oscorp running smoothly. But unfortunately for Max, her program was a bit damaged, and he needed to fix it. Which was why he was stuck at work. The typically eloquent Kari was slurring her speech.

"Bioelectrogenesis." Kari's voice came sputtering out of the speakers in the room on a loop. "The generation of electricitttytyyttyty by living organisms to fend offfffff predators. The genetically manipulated bacteriaaaaaa in this tank have been subjected to high-voltage discharge and may one day lead to saferrrrr, more efficient energy ssssssolutionnnn . . ."

Max ignored the words coming from the broken program and walked up the stairs to the top of the tank. He cracked open the electrical guts of the lab's equipment and performed a few quick tests before realizing the problem: a loose wire in one of the ducts running through the bottom of the catwalk that extended over the tank with the eels in it.

"Warning," said Kari's voice. "Warning. Malfunction in Sector 5A. Please reconnect circuit source."

"Yeah, yeah," said Max, glumly, reaching underneath the catwalk to try to open the panel and reach the loose connection. "Y'know, Kari, I just had a birthday. Be honest with you—no one remembered. You can only take so much," he vented. "A person can only take so much. I have feelings. I don't ask for a lot. Just someone to sing 'Happy Birthday' to me. Would you sing 'Happy Birthday' with me, Kari?"

The robotic voice only repeated the warning about the power malfunction. Max sang softly to himself while trying to reconnect the circuit. But Max didn't realize the problem with the power wasn't just the loose wire. . . .

The instant he reconnected the loose connection, an overload of power surged through the system, shooting electricity through Max's body. Electrified,

Max fell into the tank below, where the genetically modified eels fired off currents of their own. It was enough electricity to kill a person, but the combination of the events in the lab did something *more* to Max. As his body convulsed in the tank, the last thing he heard was Kari's voice, no longer broken or stuttering: "System restored. Have a nice day."

Uptown from the Oscorp offices, Peter Parker walked toward a gigantic and ornate apartment building.

Upstairs, Harry Osborn, the son of the late Norman Osborn, was facing down the board of Oscorp for the first time since his father's recent death. Harry was under a lot of pressure, but he was not the sort of person to back down when someone tried to pick a fight. And he certainly wasn't about to start now, on the most important day of his life so far.

"To date," one of the Oscorp lawyers droned on to the room, "Oscorp Holdings includes over two thousand proprietary patents in the areas of science and technology, as well as—"

"Bioengineering, I get it," snapped Harry. "What're all these redacted files?"

The lawyer who had been speaking looked nervously at Donald Menken, the head director of operations for Oscorp.

"Harry," Menken began, "Oscorp's been under intense public scrutiny in the wake of Dr. Connors'... breach of trust."

"You mean to say that people got mad at him after he tried to turn everyone in New York into giant lizards?" Harry asked sarcastically.

"Given that—all of the human/animal hybrid programs he was involved in were destroyed. To restore investor confidence."

"Of course," said Harry. "Because that's the Osborn way: whatever's inconvenient around here, get rid of it, right?" He stared straight at Menken. Everyone in the room knew Harry was talking about himself, but no one knew what to say. Heck, no one wanted to pick a fight with the young unstable man who had suddenly and surprisingly been placed in control of all of their jobs.

"Much of that scrutiny may fall on you now," said Menken, breaking the silence. "We felt 'plausible deniability' was your best option."

"Sure, sure, I get it. Twenty-year-old kid? Two-hundred-billion-dollar company? What was Dad thinking?" he said sharply. "I mean, you're all lawyers, right? Someone at this table must've questioned his sanity at the end." He stared directly at Menken. "*Someone* must've thought about having him declared legally incompetent. Would've made this conversation easier."

"Harry . . ."

"It's 'Mr. Osborn.' We're not friends."

He turned to address his father's former assistant, a young woman sitting across from him at the table.

"You were his assistant, right?" he asked, smiling slyly. "What's your name?"

"Felicia, sir."

"Hi."

"Hi," Felicia said, appreciatively.

The warmth immediately drained from Harry's voice as he addressed the rest of the room. "From now on, everyone here works for Felicia, because Felicia works for me. I'm running this company now. And I'm not going anywhere. Anybody wanna speak up?"

Harry's speech was met by angry faces from everyone in the room. Menken glared at Harry.

"Great," said Harry. "You can all keep your jobs a little longer."

Harry's butler then walked into the room and whispered something into Harry's ear. Surprised, Harry got up and headed out of the conference room. "I want to see every file on this list," he said before leaving the room. He pointed at the redacted list of Oscorp experiments. "Every. Single. One."

In the foyer outside the conference room, Peter Parker stood, gawking at the opulence on display.

"Peter?" said Harry. "Peter Parker?"

"Harry Osborn," Peter said. "Hi . . ."

"This is random," said Harry. "Ten years."

"Eight."

"So . . . what's up?" asked Harry suspiciously.

"I saw the news," said Peter. "I probably should've called, I just didn't know how to reach you and . . . I wanted to see if you were . . ."

"Thank you," said Harry curtly. "I'm with some people."

"Oh, all right," said Peter. "I'm . . . I can give you my number, or . . ."

Harry just stared at Peter. Peter didn't know what to say and was starting to feel like he'd made a mistake coming to Harry's ridiculously gigantic apartment in the first place.

"I don't know what you must be feeling," Peter began. "But I kinda do know what you must be feeling. And . . . you were there for me. And I wanted to do the same for you. . . . I know it's been a long time, but I'm here if you need me. I guess that's all I'm saying. I'm here."

More silence. "And . . . I'm leaving." Peter turned around and started to walk back toward the front door of the apartment. But just then, Harry's voice called out to him.

"You got your braces off."

"Uh, yeah," said Peter. "Like, seven years ago."

"Hmmm," Harry said with a smirk. "Now there's nothing to distract from your unibrow."

Peter relaxed. This was the Harry he remembered from all those years ago. "You still wake up early to blow dry your hair? Or does your manservant do it?"

"He holds the dryer, but I work the brush. I'm not *completely* spoiled. Still sleep with a blankie?"

"I weaned myself," Peter said, laughing. "I'm not saying it was easy. . . ."

Harry was surprised by how good it felt to see his old friend again. "Wanna go for a ride?" he asked Peter. "I got a new toy."

Peter wasn't sure what he'd thought Harry meant when he'd said "new toy," but he definitely wasn't expecting a high-powered speedboat. And he definitely hadn't been expecting to find himself shooting up the Hudson River with his childhood friend, bouncing through the waves at high speed.

"Brazil after graduation," Harry said, slowing down the boat while catching Peter up on the past eight-plus years. "Singapore . . . Europe . . ."

"I saw you in a magazine with that Italian super-model," said Peter, a little awestruck.

"Ugh, the whole model thing. So exhausting."

"Yeah," Peter said unsympathetically, "that must be really hard."

"You got a lady?" asked Harry.

"Hmmm? No," said Peter. "Yeah. Sort of. On again, off again. Currently off. I'm afraid of hurting her, I can't live without her, it's complicated," he rattled off quickly.

"Yeah, I don't do complicated," Harry said to Peter. "Who is she?"

"Her name's Gwen. Gwen Stacy. She's part of the work-study program at Oscorp, actually."

"Why do hot girls always have two first names?" Harry thought out loud. "Why'd you split up?"

"Kind of a conflict with my . . . job," said Peter cautiously.

"You didn't say you had a job."

"I do odd jobs," said Peter. "Photography. Some Web design."

"So, your sort-of girlfriend conflicted with your career in the odd-jobs arena?"

"See, when you say it like that, it sounds . . ."

"Like you're making yourself miserable for no reason?" said Harry with a smile. It felt good to actually talk to a friend again rather than a boardroom of stone-faced lawyers. "See, that's why I'm sticking to models."

He shifted the boat back up to full speed, and the two of them took off up the river again. They zoomed upstate a bit and docked at one of the Osborns' homes, where they continued playing catch-up. Harry finally opened up about his father.

"After my father sent me away, I tried real hard to forget everything about this place," Harry said. "I guess that sort of included you."

"You don't have to explain it to me, man," said Peter. "We both got dumped by our folks."

"Did you ever find out why your parents bailed?"

Harry asked. Their fathers had been friends and coworkers, and the mysteries they had left behind were clearly going to loom over their sons for a long time to come.

"Dad just left behind this briefcase full of clues. Notes. Papers. Something about the word 'Roosevelt,'" said Peter.

"What's that?"

"Exactly. I don't know if it's a person, a place . . ." He drifted off, getting lost in his head for a second. "I try not to think about it anymore," he said, though it was clear he thought about it all the time. The two boys climbed off the boat and began walking along the Hudson River.

Peter picked up a small rock from along the shore and flicked it out, skipping it along the water. Except, being relaxed and lost in thought, he forgot to watch his strength and sent the stone rocketing out over the water. Harry looked at him.

"Nice arm!"

"All in the, uh, wrist," Peter said, trying to play it down.

"What're you, some kinda Super Hero?"

"Yeah, me, a Super Hero," said Peter, chuckling. "Right."

"You gotta admit," said Harry, lost in his own thoughts, "things've gotten pretty crazy lately. Giant reptiles? Spider . . . guys?"

"Just one guy," Peter said quickly. "One Spider-Man. Or woman. We don't know for sure."

"Whatever," said Harry, unimpressed. "He wears spandex and rescues kittens from trees. Really?"

"I sort of like to think he gives people . . . hope?"

"For what?"

"That, eventually, everything's going to be okay."

Much later that night, in a morgue, a nondescript Oscorp employee was secretly trying to get rid of the evidence of the accident that had seemingly killed Max Dillon. He wheeled a body bag into the room.

"No autopsy report," said the man in the suit, handing a large envelope overstuffed with money to the coroner. "Once the body's incinerated, it was never here."

"I'm sorry," the coroner said greedily. "I'm looking right at it."

The suit reached into his pocket and pulled out another wad of cash, handing it over to the coroner. "I love the night shift," said the coroner as the man in the suit walked out of the room.

The coroner put a pair of headphones on and started prepping the equipment to get rid of the body. He didn't notice strange electrical events happening all around him: an electric wheelchair started moving on its own; lights on the desk behind him began to flicker; and small bolts of electricity flew around him.

He went over to open the body bag, but he was zapped with electricity from seemingly out of nowhere as soon as he touched the bag's metal zipper! His head banged against the wall, and the last thing he saw before losing consciousness was the lights flickering in the room.

He never saw the source of all of these events: Max

Dillon. It wasn't just that Max appeared unharmed from having untold amounts of electricity coursing through his veins—he seemed stronger than he had ever been!

He looked at his hands and could see pure power flowing through his veins instead of blood. Various objects flew around the room, attracted to and repelled by Max's body. A saw turned itself on and flew toward Max, and he instinctively reached a hand out to protect his face. The saw stopped, but that wasn't the most amazing part. It was that it stopped in *midair*. Max stared at the floating piece of machinery, coming to the realization that he was the one controlling it. How was this happening? How did he get here? Where was "here"? He stumbled out of the room and into the night.

Peter Parker sat down in a waiting room in the Oscorp offices, a place that always made him feel more than a little strange. Oscorp was where he'd been bitten by the genetically altered spider that gave him his powers, and walking through the front doors always reminded him of the dangers and opportunities the building presented to people. But there wasn't time to think about any of that now. He was mainly wondering why Harry Osborn, his old friend and the new head of the company, had asked Peter to meet him.

"Mr. Parker?" said Felicia to Peter, noticing the lost look on his face. "Are you all right?"

"Uh, yeah. Fine. Hi," Peter said, confused.

"I'm Mr. Osborn's executive assistant," said Felicia. "He's expecting you. Follow me?"

Peter walked into Harry's office, which was bustling with activity. Most of it centered on a man who looked like a soldier dressed in something that could only be called a power suit—a series of linked pieces of armor. The man was followed by a small squadron of people with tablets and clipboards, asking questions and taking notes.

"Righteous, huh?" Harry exclaimed. "New military body-armor prototype." He looked as if he hadn't slept in a week and like he'd maybe had a few too many cups of coffee. He had a small rubber ball in one hand, and he bounced it off of the walls and the floor in a chaotic pattern.

"Wow," said Peter, looking wide-eyed at the power armor. "Amazing joint flexibility. They using servomotors?"

"Electrically conductive nanofibers."

"Right, sure. Polymetric or carbon?"

"Both!" Harry said excitedly, continuing to bounce his ball around the room. "It's the next-next gen—any battlefield injury, broken leg, gunshot wound, the suit pretty much does the walking for you while it heals your body."

Harry, Peter, and Felicia all walked over to the window with a giant view of the Oscorp hydroelectric power plant and the Manhattan skyline.

"What do you think?" Harry asked, pointing out the window. "A view of my very own power plant! Am I lucky or what?" He seemed to be getting more jittery by the second. He fired his rubber ball too hard at a priceless vase, which instantly shattered. The ball bounced back up, almost hitting Felicia, as well. But Peter reached his hand out faster than anyone could see and snagged the ball inches away from Felicia's face.

"Whoopsie," said Harry.

"I'll have someone clean that up, sir," said Felicia. It seemed like she'd already gotten used to Harry's energetic bursts.

"Not now, Felicia," said Harry, sitting down. "Be a lamb and hold my calls, would you?"

"Of course, Mr. Osborn," Felicia said, walking out of the office and closing the door behind her.

"You okay, Harry?" Peter asked, looking concerned.

"Not really, Pete," Harry confessed, looking haggard. "I'm dying. But I think you can help save my life. . . ."

Peter looked up, bewildered. Dying? Why hadn't Harry told him before?

Harry explained to Peter about the rare disease his father had, for which he'd tried desperately to find a cure. Eventually, it took his father's life. It was also slowly but surely destroying Harry as well.

"My dad left me all his files," he continued. "Everything he'd been working on. I found one labeled PETER, and I think you need to see what's in it."

Harry pressed a button; a multitude of pictures appeared on a giant screen, all scenes from Peter's past—his childhood, him with Aunt May and Uncle Ben. Peter was stunned and astonished.

"What . . . what is this?!"

"He had you and your aunt and uncle under surveillance. Crazy, right? He spent more time watching you than me," Harry said bitterly.

Peter just stared at the screen, thinking a million thoughts at once. But he could only get out one question: "Why?"

"Isn't that the question of the day?" Harry said calmly. "Aunt May and Uncle Ben ever tell you anything?"

"No . . ." Peter knew he needed more information—but he had to be very, very careful about how he asked. "How long was he watching us?"

"Eight years," Harry said. "But it looks like nothing

ever came of it, so he gave up. Gets better, though. Our fathers made this when they started their work together."

He pushed another button, and a video of a young Richard Parker and a young Norman Osborn came up on the screen. Peter's father spoke to the camera.

"The common household spider: unlike humans, their cells contain the power to self-heal from infection or tissue damage. We've used a radioactive isotope to genetically engineer these 'super' spiders with compatible human DNA."

"You're looking at the world's first human/spider hybrids," said Norman Osborn. "Brought to you by Oscorp."

"The hope," said Richard, "is to extract the venom from their glands and turn it into a cure that heals diseased cells. . . ."

"Like mine," Norman finished. "And if I can be cured, imagine what this could do for other diseases— like high blood pressure, Alzheimer's, even cancer."

"We're calling it the Double Zero Project," said Richard proudly. "Two zeroes, for 'infinity.'"

THE AMAZING SPIDER-MAN is ready for anything swinging his way!

On his way to his high school graduation, Spider-Man stops a bunch of **MOBSTERS IN A STOLEN TRUCK**.

WOW! Max cannot believe he just met his idol, Spider-Man, who tells Max: "You're my eyes and ears out there. I need you, okay?"

AFTER GWEN BREAKS UP WITH PETER, Spidey continues to watch over her and make sure she is safe.

After his shocking accident, Max's life is *CHANGED FOREVER*.

CONFUSED AND LOST, Max roams the streets of New York only to find himself in the heart of Times Square!

Soon, Max realizes his new **ELECTRIFYING POWERS** and he can't help himself from testing them out . . . on Spidey!

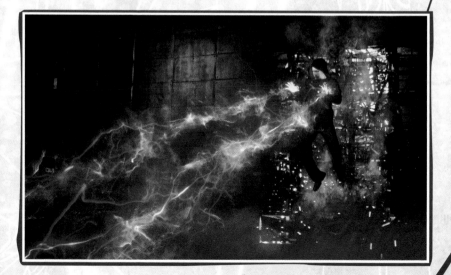

MAX CAUSES HAVOC and destoys jumbotrons with the flick of a wrist.

SPIDER-MAN swings over just in time to rescue innocent bystanders in Times Square from Max's rage.

After saving the day, Spidey watches over as this new enemy is lead away . . . **BUT TO WHERE**?

Peter tries to piece together what happened to his parents the night they **DISAPPEARED**.

When Harry frees Max from Ravencroft, Max decides to go by **ELECTRO**.

Determined, Peter works hard on his new **WEB-SHOOTERS** in order defeat the Super Villain, Electro.

HAS SPIDEY MET HIS MATCH? The battle with Electro starts now!

Harry paused the video.

"They never even made it to human trials," said Harry. "So my father ran out of hope . . . and time. Fourteen years of research and nothing to show for it." He picked up the newest copy of *The Daily Bugle*, with a picture of Spider-Man on the front page. "Except maybe this: Spider-Man," he said.

CHAPTER 4
LIGHTS, CAMERA . . . ACTION

"I'M MOVING TO ENGLAND," Gwen
Stacy announced.

Peter Parker gaped at the gorgeous woman in front
of him, his soul mate, his everything. Sure, they hadn't
spoken to each other since they'd broken up a year
earlier. And sure, the only contact they'd had since
that fateful night had been Peter keeping a watchful
eye on Ms. Stacy from above the city streets without
her knowing it. But she hadn't made this date out of
the blue just to tell him she was leaving . . . had she?

"Um . . . what?" Peter mustered.

"I got this scholarship to Oxford in molecular
medicine. Well, I didn't exactly get it yet. The final

round's an oral exam, and it's between me and this other kid from India."

"That's . . . England. . . ." echoed Peter.

Gwen smiled. "Yeah, you know, the Queen? Double-decker buses? Mint jelly? I can go on."

"Uh, no. Gwen, that's an incredible opportunity. Honestly. Congratulations. I . . ."

Suddenly, Peter's spider-sense tingled. Something was going on. Something more pressing than his true love moving across the ocean. Evidently, this conversation would have to wait. He looked up, trying to home in on the exact location of the trouble.

"What's wrong?" Gwen asked.

A street lamp flickered; in an instant, Gwen was alone. She found Peter's jacket, shirt, and backpack in her arms. The street was deserted.

Well, that went well, she thought.

Max Dillon staggered toward Times Square. It had been a rough day, considering he'd fallen into a vat of electric eels and had woken up in the morgue. He felt so strange. So shaken. So . . . *thirsty*.

Max stumbled to a steel grate. Propelled by an odd urge, he wrapped his fingers through the mesh and tore the grate off with surprising strength. A shock ran through his body. Amazingly enough, it didn't hurt one bit. It just sort of tingled, encouraging him to continue. Snapping the lock off the junction box, Max pulled one of the live cables free. Forty thousand volts of electricity surged into him, quenching his thirst. He greedily lapped up every volt. Better. That was *much* better.

"FREEZE!"

Max turned to see a flock of police officers, all pointing their guns at him. Max's glowing eyes widened in fear. What was going on?

Strangely, the officers looked just as nervous as Max. He raised his hands in the air. Why were they after him? He hadn't done anything. He slowly started backing away and found himself in the middle of the street, directly in the path of a speeding delivery truck.

Max reflexively threw his hands in front of him,

trying to brace himself for the impending impact. Bolts of electricity shot from his fingertips. The delivery truck flipped away from Max and skidded on its side.

How did . . . ?

Suddenly, chaos ensued. Passersby started running in all directions. In what seemed like seconds, the scene was filled with news vans, SWAT team members, and helicopters.

"Down on the ground, or we'll open fire!" shouted the SWAT team leader.

"Stop! It's not my fault!" Max yelled back. Why wasn't anybody listening to him? He just wanted to go home.

Just then, a flash of light passed across his face. Max looked up to see a luminescent man in a black hoodie broadcast on the jumbotrons. Wait . . . that was *him*! Time seemed to slow down as delirious thoughts drifted into Max's head. *Everyone sees me. Everyone. I look so . . . powerful.* Like a glowing Narcissus, Max was mesmerized by his reflection. *What am I?*

A loud clanking interrupted Max's stupor. He looked down to see metal canisters on the ground beside him—gas grenades. Sweeping his hands through the air, he cleared the paralyzing smoke.

"I said stop!" Max threw the cans back at the SWAT vans, where they bounced and ricocheted into the crowd. Fine. They weren't going to play nice and listen? It was time to *make* them listen. A giant sphere of energy started growing around Max—it was like his body knew exactly what to do. He blasted the energy toward the police cars, flipping them wildly in random directions. One of the cars clipped a fire hydrant, spraying water into a quickly widening pool.

The SWAT team opened fire, but Max incinerated the bullets midair with his energy pulse. He'd never felt so alive.

"Eagle Eye, do you have the shot?" the SWAT leader yelled into his radio.

"Negative. Too much smoke," the chopper sniper replied.

Max flipped another incoming cop car, spinning it

skyward. As it nosedived, an officer looked up to see the car about to smash him. But at the last possible second, the car stopped midair.

"You probably want to *move*," grunted a voice from underneath the car. The officer scurried away just as Spider-Man set the vehicle down. The web-slinger leaped up onto the hood.

"Need a hand?" he asked the SWAT team leader.

"This is a police matter," the leader replied sternly.

"Oh, okay. I've got super-strength, and I'm a Super Hero, but you guys look like you got this under control. I'll just go home?"

The SWAT team leader sighed. "Attention, all teams," he called into his radio as Spider-Man strolled into the middle of Times Square. "Spider-Man's going in to negotiate. Hold your fire until my signal."

"Yo, Sparkles!" Spidey said to the shining maniac causing all the fuss.

Max whirled around, stunned to see his hero right in front of him. "It's you!"

"I know it's me. Who are *you*?" Spider-Man asked.

"You . . . you don't remember me?"

Spider-Man paused. "Should I?"

"You saved my life. I stepped into the street, that truck almost hit me. . . ."

The realization suddenly dawned on Spider-Man—the timid man with his hands full, the hijacked van speeding toward him. "You're the guy with the blueprints. . . ."

"Yeah . . ."

What happened to this guy? the wall-crawler thought. Aloud, he asked, "What's your name again?"

"Max."

"Good to see you, Max." Spider-Man extended his hand.

Max gaped at the hero, unsure what to do. Spider-Man looked down to see the pool of water spreading toward the metal grate next to the set of bleachers that stood in the heart of Times Square. Sparks of electricity sputtered alarmingly off Max. It would be only a matter of time before a spark, the water, and the grate conducted a perfect storm of deadly energy up into the bleachers . . . and the many tourists sitting there, terrified and fascinated by the action.

Spider-Man had to lead Max away from the grate.

"I don't know what's happening to me," Max said incredulously.

"I believe you."

"Y-you do?" Max stuttered.

Spider-Man inched his way closer to Max. "You're one of the good guys. I don't think you want to hurt anyone. I know what it's like to be misunderstood. Why don't you step back from that grate, and let's get out of here? You can tell me everything, okay?"

Max remained glued to his spot. Sparks jumped from his feet toward the metal grate . . . and the water creeping closer to it.

"All I ever wanted was for people to see me," he said, laughing as he looked down at his glowing body.

"They do, Max," Spider-Man replied seriously.

"Do they? Do they really?" Max looked up at his hero, needing to hear it.

A blinding light suddenly interrupted the scene. A tourist on the bleachers had snapped a photo, causing Max to jump and shoot a burst of electricity out of his fingertips.

Fearing another electrical attack, the SWAT team jumped into action.

"Take the shot now!" the SWAT leader yelled.

Bullets pelted down toward Max.

"No! Stop!" Spider-Man shouted at the circling chopper.

Enraged, Max fired two more bolts at the helicopter.

Oh, no, you don't. Come on, Max, Spider-Man thought as he rapidly fired off a web-line to stop the bolts midair. ZZZZTT. The web conducted the massive amounts of electricity right back to Spider-Man, slamming him into a cop car.

Dazed, Spider-Man glanced at his wrist. *Great.* The web-shooter was fried. He'd have to make his remaining good one count.

He looked up just in time to see Max's energy waves hit a towering building nearby, creating a sea of debris that plummeted toward the screaming civilians below. *You're not really helping yourself here, buddy,* Spider-Man thought grimly.

"Ahhhh!"

The web-slinger focused on a slim man who'd been knocked down by those fleeing around him. A falling piece of metal sped toward him. Before the man could be crushed, Spider-Man shot a web and yanked him to safety.

In a flash, the jumbotrons displayed Spider-Man carrying the man to safety. "Spidey! Spidey! Spidey!" the crowd cheered.

Led by the chants, Gwen Stacy rushed down the busy street and pushed her way toward the front of the police barricade. "Peter," she whispered, her eyes widening at the hectic scene displayed by the jumbotrons.

Max, too, glanced up at the giant screens. Spider-Man. He'd been . . . replaced. Betrayed. By the one who was supposed to be on *his* side. Max's face darkened with fury.

"You're a liar!" he screamed at Spider-Man. "You just told me what I wanted to hear!"

"No, Max. Stay with me," Spider-Man said. "I wasn't trying to hurt you."

Caught up in a blind rage, Max slammed his hands on the metal grate. The electric charge formed ripples in the water, racing toward the bleachers. Spider-Man turned to see the crowd about to be electrocuted by the incoming pulse. With his remaining web-shooter, Spider-Man lassoed hands, feet, and bags, yanking the tourists off the red-and-white stands one by one. He bounded up the bleachers, sprinting just ahead of the deadly shock wave. Finally, he grabbed the one last man on the bleachers. It was the tourist with the camera, frozen in fear. The web-slinger lifted the man in his arms.

"Smile!" Spidey joked as the stunned tourist regained his composure enough to snap a shot with his hero before Spider-Man placed him back on the ground.

Max, on the other hand, had lost his hero. He started throwing bolts at Spider-Man. The web-slinger leaped around the square, dodging the blasts.

"Guess what, Spidey?" Max continued, shooting a stream of energy bolts. "You were my hero, but you're just like the rest of them!"

"You're going to get people killed!" Spider-Man tried to appeal to the last bit of humanity in Max.

"Maybe they don't deserve to live!" Max screamed as he levitated himself into the air.

"Wrong choice," Spider-Man said, webbing a fire hydrant and whipping it around in a wide circle. One of Max's blasts hit him just as he let it go, and the hydrant hurtled straight into Max.

"Ahhhhhh!" Max shrieked as he flew back into the jumbotron high above Times Square. The screen exploded in a shower of sparks that rained down to the street below. Remarkably, Max didn't feel any pain. He was all right. *Better than all right,* he thought, noticing a loose cable buzzing beside him. *More. Power.* He sucked the energy from the cable into his body until every screen in Times Square exploded. Then he levitated off the steel frame, electrical particles swirling around him.

Gwen gasped from down below. "He uses power . . ."

". . . to regenerate," Spider-Man concluded at the same time.

Meanwhile, the jumbotron's frame started to

topple off its base. The crowd gasped as the support beams creaked and started to give way.

Max gazed down at the mayhem from his perch above the jumbotron's steel skeleton. The metal acted as a counter-magnet. Electricity arched under his feet and acted as a solid place to stand. *So that's why he can fly!* Spidey thought. He drifted over the street, hovering like a dark angel, a hungry look in his eye. He would teach them. All of them. They would listen to him. And now they would definitely know his name.

A loud hissing sound erupted in the air. Suddenly, Max was blasted by a flood of water. Spider-Man held a fire hose, spraying Max until he shorted out. He crashed to the ground, electric bolts arcing wildly off his body.

"Game over," Spider-Man announced as men from the Ravencroft Institute for the Criminally Insane loaded the unconscious Max into their van.

Just another night for your friendly neighborhood Spider-Man.

The wall-crawler headed toward the barricade, stopping in front of Gwen.

They looked at each other for a second. Then Spider-Man broke the tension.

"So, England?"

Gwen smirked.

CHAPTER 5
HERO OR ZERO?

"**ONLINE POLLS** show a sudden uptick in public sentiment in favor of Spider-Man. After tonight's scare in Times Square, it would seem New York owes him a debt of gratitude."

Peter gave a wan smile at the newscaster as he switched off the TV. It felt good to be appreciated. He glanced around his darkened room, looking for something to do. His eyes fell on the cell phone resting idly on his desk. Peter flipped it open, illuminating the screen.

The one and only Gwen Stacy smiled back at him. Peter snapped the phone shut. Nope. Thinking about

Gwen leaving for England was not how he wanted to spend his evening.

Peter flopped onto the bed, blasting music in his earbuds and closing his eyes. Why couldn't he turn off his brain? His eyes fluttered open and zeroed in on his closet with the open door. And then on his dad's briefcase that sat right there on the floor. Nope. He wasn't going to think about his parents, either. Or how he knew there was more to their sudden deaths than anyone was saying. Or that every time he brought it up to Aunt May, she abruptly changed the subject. He tried shutting his eyes once more, but the briefcase nagged at him.

Peter stormed toward the closet, slamming the door closed. He took a few steps back and then stopped. *Forget it,* Peter thought.

But he wasn't getting any peace that night. He doubled back and yanked the closet door open. In one swift motion, he grabbed the briefcase and dumped its contents onto his desk.

A slew of unremarkable items formed a pile. A

folder with the Oscorp twin-circles logo on it. A calculator. A subway token. A handwritten reminder about some random appointment. There had to be a clue in there somewhere. Peter sighed and pulled at one of his desk drawers, finding an old framed photo of him and his parents smiling happily in their living room.

He vaguely remembered that day. It'd been a rough afternoon for him. Something about not being able to figure out a key detail for his accelerated-science class project—those details were fuzzy now. But he could still vividly see his dad tousling his hair and smiling down at him. "You know," his dad had said. "Every problem has a solution. Sometimes you just have to let it reveal itself."

With a renewed sense of determination, Peter taped the photo to his wall. Then he hopped onto his computer, typing various search terms frantically. Seconds later, his printer started spitting out pages of maps. Pinning them to the wall, he started highlighting routes, drawing arrows, trying to connect the dots.

Where were you going? he scribbled on scraps of paper. *Who were you running from? Why???* He posted these, as well.

Finally, he ran out of steam. Stepping back, he stared at the obsession wall he'd made, willing the answers to jump out at him. Nada. He cocked his head. Anything from this angle? Not even a hint.

Well, it was a start. Maybe the solution would reveal itself later.

Grabbing his fried shooter, he headed to the garage. At least the case of the electrocuted web-shooter was one problem he could solve.

Soon, Peter was blaring rock music from the old-school boom box on Uncle Ben's workbench, a box of homemade web-shooters stationed close by.

Peter examined the broken shooter. The battle with Max had destroyed it. There had to be some way to shield it from electric currents. Though Max was locked away at Ravencroft now, there was no way Peter would want a repeat from some other nut job out to play Shock the Spider.

Peter searched the web for "electrical insulators." He scrolled through the results: rubber . . . ceramics . . . Bingo. Rummaging through the workbench supplies, he found what he was looking for.

Thwip. He shot a web to the wall with his good web-shooter, and then plugged in a portable generator. Tearing off a length of electrical tape, he wrapped it around the shooter. Perfect. Peter removed its nickel-lithium battery, tweaked the wiring, and attached it to a D battery. *That should do the trick,* he thought.

Pulling out jumper cables, he clamped one end to the generator and taped the other end to the web.

"Here we go," he said as he started the generator.

ZZZZZZT! Sparks flew as electricity arced along the web, and . . . *POP.* The shooter exploded. Peter pulled the blackened D battery from the wreckage, eyeing it closely.

"We're going to need a bigger battery," he mused.

An hour later, batteries of various volts and sizes had succumbed to the same fate. As a last resort, he sprayed the web with some of Aunt May's hairspray.

This should insulate it. . . . The web burst into flames as soon as he attached the jumper cable. *Aunt May is not going to be happy*, Peter thought as the smell of fried wiring filled the air.

Coughing, Peter grabbed the fire extinguisher and foamed the fire.

It was going to be a long night.

Days later, Spider-Man saw himself holding up a deli delivery guy. That is, he saw a thief dressed in a make-shift Spidey outfit. The delivery guy was frozen in front of an apartment building, his tray of cold cuts shaking.

"Give me your money! Let's go," the thief growled, shoving his gun in the man's face.

"Wow. It's like staring into a mirror," the web-slinger observed.

The thief looked up in alarm, seeing the real Spider-Man hanging upside down from a fire escape.

"A shorter, fatter mirror," Spider-Man continued

as he shot a web and yanked the thief off his feet. He shot another web, which coiled around the man's hand, and yanked his gun away.

BANG! The gun went off instantly, prompting the terrified deliveryman to throw his platter of food into the air. As soon as Spidey caught the gun, he was showered with a mixture of cold cuts and coleslaw.

"Uh . . . thanks, man. Sorry," the delivery guy said awkwardly.

Spider-Man sighed and wiped the dripping cabbage off his mask. "Next time? Hold the slaw."

As he turned to go, he felt something squishy give way underneath one of his feet. A distinctly pungent smell wafted its way up to his nostrils. *Oh, no. Don't tell me . . .* the wall-crawler thought.

"HA!"

Spider-Man looked up to see a burly New Yorker leaning out of his window and aiming his camera phone to get a candid shot. "Spider-Man stepped in dog poop!"

Things went much the same during the next few

weeks for the web-slinger. Not the right way. Talk about bad luck!

Night after night, he returned home, exhausted, covered in everything from bright blue paint to burn marks to seaweed.

It was really no wonder why he got a terrible head cold. Or why he found himself in his neighborhood bodega one night looking for the right combination of medicine that would make his fever and sore throat miraculously disappear.

"Give me all your money!"

He heard a gruff voice from the front of the market.

Peter sighed, unzipping his backpack and reaching for his mask. *I guess duty calls even when you can't breathe through your nose,* he thought ruefully.

The scruffy-haired robber pulled a gun from his jacket. The cashier gave a startled yelp and started emptying the register. He threw wads of cash to the robber.

"I know you got more in the safe!" the robber

shouted, ramming his gun in the cashier's face.

Suddenly, the gun was yanked from the robber's hand by a web. The robber turned to see Spider-Man standing right beside him. Or rather, a Spider-Man mask worn by someone in street clothes.

"What is it with you guys?" Spidey felt like an elephant was stomping on his head. Stupid congestion. "Don't you ever learn?"

The man threw a punch, which Spider-Man easily dodged, then webbed the robber's wrists to the fridge. The man sputtered in pain and struggled against the strength of the web.

Spider-Man set the gun on the counter and then put his selection of medicine down next to it.

"How mush?" he asked stuffily.

"Free! Free, man. Take it. Thank you," the bodega cashier answered hastily. "You're that spider guy!"

"Pida-Mam," Spidey corrected.

"Huh?"

"Spida-Mam," he said, trying again.

"Uh . . . what?"

Spider-Man sneezed violently inside his mask.

"Bless you?" the cashier offered, wincing a little.

Spider-Man knew when it was time to walk away. "Hab a good night."

On his way out, he noticed the latest copy of *The Daily Bugle* on the stands. The front page featured a lame picture of him with the headline HERO OR ZERO? Underneath it, a poll concluded: LIKE 47%, DISLIKE 53%. *Looks like things are back to normal,* he thought, sighing.

Lately, being a Super Hero wasn't all it was cracked up to be.

CHAPTER 6
IT'S COMPLICATED

HARRY OSBORN was a number of things. A sick friend. A millionaire. A man on a mission. Unfortunately, Peter was figuring out what that mission was. And just why he'd been invited to Harry's Oscorp office.

". . . human and spider hybrids! Just think of it—curing high blood pressure, Alzheimer's, cancer, and *my father, if he were still alive*—all by creating super insects," Harry was saying animatedly.

Peter knew that his dad and Norman Osborn had been experimenting on radioactive spiders. And it seemed Harry had just gotten in the loop.

"They never made it to human trials. So my

father ran out of hope . . . and time. Fourteen years of research and nothing to show for it." He grabbed the copy of *The Daily Bugle* on his desk. "Except maybe this."

Peter reluctantly glanced at the front page, knowing what was coming next.

"Spider-Man," Harry concluded.

"Wha—what about him?" Peter asked in what he hoped was a casual manner.

Harry laughed bitterly. "Come on. This guy sticks to walls, he spins webs, he even calls himself 'Spider-Man.' He was bitten by one of these things, and it worked. I don't know how, and I don't know why, but he can do everything a spider can. Including self-heal. I need to find him. I need his blood."

Thoughts raced through Peter's head. Of course he wanted to help Harry. But he knew that the radioactive spider was specifically coded to his DNA. Giving his blood to Harry could be disastrous. "You . . . want Spider-Man's blood?"

"It'll save my life," Harry said simply.

"Harry, it's not that easy. You saw what happened

to Connors," Peter said, referencing their fathers' former colleague who'd ended up turning into the gigantic, murderous Lizard by experimenting with lizard and human DNA transfers.

"Connors was insane," Harry replied. "He was weak. This is *me*, Peter." He paused, and then leaned closer to Peter. "I want Spider-Man."

"Uh, I don't think you can just set up a van and have him donate, you know? He's probably pretty sensitive about—"

"Oh, is he? Is he sensitive?" Harry interjected. "Well, maybe you could sensitively tell me who he is, and I'll just go ask him myself."

Peter stared at Harry, unsure how to respond.

"You took his picture. You know him. You're the only one who knows him," Harry continued, pointing to the photo credit in the newspaper.

"That's just . . . I was . . . using a long lens," Peter sputtered.

"I put together what you said at the river. About how he gives people hope? At first, I thought it was you." Harry suddenly chortled at the idea. "No offense, but you're hardly living like a big famous Super Hero. Otherwise, you would've moved out of your aunt's house in Queens. Your life's a mess, Peter. I can change all of that."

A surge of anger raced through Peter. "You know what?" he said, raising his voice. "I'm doing okay. So's my aunt. So don't worry about us."

"We can help each other," Harry offered calmly. "I know deep down, some part of you thinks that this should all be yours."

Peter's hands started to shake.

"But we can literally change the world now. *This* is why we came back into each other's lives. It's our destiny to be all the things they tried to be—failed to be. Just say yes," Harry said, more manic with every word.

Looking away, Peter willed himself to calm down. *This is your friend,* he thought. *He is not well. He doesn't understand.*

Harry grabbed Peter's arm aggressively, impatient for his response. "Don't turn your back on me. Just tell me what you want."

Peter looked up and spoke in a low, controlled voice. "I want you to let go of my arm."

Harry realized he'd taken it too far. He was pushing away his only friend . . . and his only chance at survival.

"I don't wanna end up like him, Pete," Harry said, his voice breaking. "I can't. Please."

All the anger left Peter's body as he looked at Harry's desperate expression. He had to do something. He couldn't just let his friend die. "I'll find Spider-Man," he said finally. "I'll try."

Gwen sighed and stared absently at her Oscorp computer screen. Could it be possible that the crazy guy shooting electricity from his hands in Times Square was the same timid fellow employee she'd met in the elevator?

What was his name . . . Max . . . Deacon? No, Dillon. Max Dillon. Gwen performed a search on the Oscorp database.

YOUR SEARCH HAS PRODUCED NO RESULTS.

Huh. Gwen tried various spellings and even searched "hydroelectric power," the project Max had enthusiastically told her about.

YOUR SEARCH HAS PRODUCED NO RESULTS.

"What did they do to you, Max?" Gwen muttered under her breath.

Suddenly, she noticed a flicker of movement reflecting off her monitor. Looking closer, she saw it was a conspicuous man in a black suit, quickly striding toward her. Instinctively, Gwen rose and darted away from her cube. The guy, and the fact that he was heading in her direction just as she was investigating Max Dillon's mysteriously missing files, made her leery. And she'd been through too much not to trust her instincts.

Gwen suddenly ran into a familiar face.

"What are you doing here?" Gwen and Peter asked each other simultaneously. Peter knew she was in a part of the building she shouldn't be in, and so did Gwen.

Knowing there was no time to play catch-up as the man in the black suit walked closer, Gwen pulled Peter into an adjacent supply closet and closed the door noiselessly behind them.

"There was an accident in the genomics lab, and they're covering it up," Gwen explained hurriedly. "The guy from Times Square, I *met* him in the elevator. He was just so . . . sweet. And sad. And, by the way, he loves Spider-Man."

Peter snorted. "I didn't get the love vibe. I got a wants-to-kill-me vibe."

"Yeah, that's what it's like to love you," Gwen teased. "Anyway, I came here to find out what happened to him, but he's not in the files at all. It's like he was *erased*. And now it seems Oscorp doesn't like my digging, and some guy is following me." She paused. "What are you doing here, anyway?"

Peter sighed, thinking of the more-than-awkward conversation he'd had moments ago with his former best friend. "Harry. He's dying, and he thinks my blood's the only thing that can save his life. But for all I know, it could kill him."

"Or something worse," Gwen added.

Peter shifted uncomfortably, looking over his shoulder for the man in the black suit. "They'll find us here. I'll distract them. Get to the elevator. . . ."

Gwen was about to open the door when Peter stopped her. "About England . . ."

She turned and kissed him without thinking. Peter grinned, and Gwen strode out of the supply closet, her heels clicking loudly on the floor.

From the closet doorway, Peter spied the man in the black suit spot Gwen from down the hallway. The man made a beeline for her.

Moving stealthily, Peter zipped from the supply closet and shot a web, snagging a steaming coffee mug from a desk nearby. He watched Gwen press the elevator button at the other end of the hall. Mr. Black Suit was not far behind her.

SPLASH. Peter rushed forward and flung the steaming coffee on the man. He wiped it off dramatically as the elevator doors closed, Ms. Stacy safely behind them.

"So sorry about that, man," Peter said, patting the guy down. "Hey, you work out? CrossFit?"

Mr. Black Suit looked none too pleased by the interruption to his stalking, but Peter kept babbling.

Meanwhile, Gwen breathed a sigh of relief.

But a voice sounding from the other side of the elevator made her jump.

"I'm Harry, an old friend of Peter's."

Gwen looked over at the guy leaning casually against the wall. The hair on the back of her neck rose, and she shivered reflexively.

"I know who you are. . . . Hi," she said.

"I heard you broke up."

Gwen bit her lip. "It's . . ."

". . . complicated," Harry finished for her.

"Yeah," she responded.

"Everything's always 'complicated' for Peter," Harry said grimly. "That's why he needs you. To help make his choices clear."

Gwen stared at Harry, unsure how to respond. Luckily, a *ding* sounded and the elevator doors suddenly opened.

She stepped out, resisting the urge to look back.

As she headed outside, she thought more about Peter and the incredible burdens he had to bear. She had a feeling he was in over his head. So she was determined to lend him a hand. She knew she had to help him, no matter what. Because *that was* what it was like to love him.

CHAPTER 7
IT'S NOT FAIR

AN EVENING BREEZE wafted through the curtains, rustling the fast-food wrappers among the pizza boxes and half-empty bottles in the messy room.

Harry Osborn shifted, uncomfortable in his sleeping position on the floor of his father's study. *His* study. He had to get used to the fact that his father was gone. Everything that had once belonged to his father—the estate, Oscorp, even the disease that killed him—was now Harry's.

"I think you're looking for me."

Harry squinted up to see a masked figure hanging upside down from the ceiling. Perhaps under normal circumstances, he would have been startled to see Spider-Man in his house in the middle of the night. But these circumstances were anything but normal.

"How'd you get in?" Harry asked quietly.

"I'm a Super Hero," Spider-Man replied.

"Must be nice."

"Also, you left the window open," Spidey added, gesturing toward the offending window.

Harry kept his eyes on Spider-Man. "I gotta stop doing that." Then, in the same breath, he asked, "Did you talk to Peter?"

Spider-Man dropped from the ceiling with the grace and ease of a cat. Harry, on the other hand, stumbled to his feet.

The reality of the situation was sinking in for the young millionaire. Peter had done it. Somehow Peter had gotten ahold of Spider-Man and told him how badly Harry needed him, how Harry believed that the hero was the only one who could cure his life-threatening disease. And now the wall-crawler was actually there . . . and he was taking an awfully long time to answer his question.

"I want to help you, Mr. Osborn. I really do."
Spider-Man paused, thinking of how best to phrase
what he wanted to say. "But I can't give you my blood."

Harry looked blankly at Spider-Man. Then he
erupted with a dark chuckle.

Spider-Man continued, choosing to ignore
Harry's unnerving reaction. "It's too dangerous. Your
body could reject it. If our blood isn't compatible, it
could *kill* you."

"That's my choice," Harry responded passionately,
instantly dropping the cavalier attitude. "I'm already
dying. Your blood can't make me die more."

"It could do something worse."

Harry considered this, and then it dawned on
him. *This guy's playing hardball.*

"How much?" he asked the web-slinger. "I'll pay
you whatever you want. You like boats? How about a
plane?"

Spider-Man sighed. "I don't want your money."

"Everyone wants my money." It was a simple state-
ment, but both men could feel the weight of those
words.

"No . . . no . . ." Spider-Man started gently, unsure how to proceed.

Harry just stared. He'd been betrayed. By Peter and by this stupid masked freak. Rage, bitter disappointment, and desperation started to build up inside of him. He staggered toward Spider-Man with a dangerous, dark glint in his eye.

"So . . . that's it? You're just going to let me die?"

"I want to help you find another way," Spidey responded. "I'm trying to protect you."

Harry raised his voice. "No. You're trying to protect yourself. You just want to be the only Super Hero around here."

"I just need to figure something out."

"I DON'T HAVE TIME!" Harry exploded with fury. He swung at Spider-Man, who easily dodged the punch. Harry lost his balance and fell to the floor. Spidey looked down miserably at his friend. It was torture to see him in that kind of pain.

"Please," he said, walking toward Harry in an attempt to comfort him. "Don't do this."

"I swear to God, I will END you!" Harry grabbed

a decanter from an oak table and swung it at the hero. Again, Spidey easily flipped out of the way. Propelled by his momentum, Harry crashed into a cabinet. Warm, iron-tasting blood spilled from his bottom lip. Humiliated and enraged, he turned, ready to lunge at the wall-crawler once more.

But the room was suddenly very empty. Spider-Man had gone.

"IT'S NOT FAIR! IT'S NOT FAIR!" Harry screamed over and over again. He went on a rampage, tearing up trash, books, pillows . . . everything in sight.

Meanwhile, Spider-Man clung to the outside of the building, just above the open window. He debated going back in to try to calm down his friend. But no . . . What Harry needed was another option. Something Harry—and Spider-Man—would have to figure out as soon as possible. Heartsick and determined, Spidey swung away from the Osborn estate and into the night.

Later that night, Harry was furtively scrolling through the files on his father's high-tech glass desktop, redirecting his energy toward last-ditch efforts to find a cure. There had to be something he was missing in the vast Oscorp database. Something that could be useful.

A folder called "Special Projects" caught his eye. As soon as he selected it, hundreds of files popped up, including a recent one marked "Yesterday." What the heck could that be?

Harry clicked through the contents.

EMPLOYEE FILE DETECTION: DILLON, MAX

ALIAS: ELECTRO

SUBJECT: INDUSTRIAL ACCIDENT

Harry opened a video attached to the file. He saw a bespectacled employee tinkering with the wiring in an Oscorp chemical genomics lab. He watched the employee—who must have been Max Dillon—appear to get electrocuted and then fall straight into a tank of electric eels.

Harry was stunned. How had this happened? Why

hadn't he been notified immediately? And how had this not been all over the news?

Another few lines caught his eye:

PATIENT TRANSFERRED TO RAVENCROFT INSTITUTE FOR THE CRIMINALLY INSANE ID 696 APPROVED BY OSBORN, HARRY

He hadn't approved this. He hadn't even *seen* this. And how could Max Dillon be transferred anywhere? He shouldn't have survived the accident.

Harry clicked another attached video and saw the same employee, only this time the guy appeared bulked up and . . . glowing. Whoa. Max Dillon really was "Electro" now. He was also suspended by wires over another tank and hooked up to dozens of machines. And he was screaming.

"I'm going to kill the light so everyone knows what it's like to live in my world. A world without power! A world without kindness! A world without Spider-Man!"

Harry blinked, trying to process what he'd just witnessed.

Just then, the files closed automatically and a security message popped up on the screen:

WARNING: YOUR USER ACCESS HAS BEEN REVOKED.

The door to the office burst open, and Menken entered with an entourage of security officers and men in black suits, Felicia trailing behind them.

"Mr. Osborn, he just barged right past," Felicia explained hurriedly.

Harry stood up from the desk, clenching his fists. "What did you do?" he demanded of Oscorp's director of operations and his father's closest advisor. He'd never exactly trusted the guy, but he didn't think he was capable of pulling something as underhanded as this.

"The more relevant question is, what did *you* do?" Menken replied evenly. "An employee was killed, and your first act as CEO was to cover it up."

Harry could not believe his ears. Another betrayal. Menken had probably been planning this mutiny all along, finding just the right event to pin on Harry so he could be ousted quickly and easily. He felt like a chump.

"You covered it up and buried him in that big house using my name."

Menken smiled. "Ravencroft is a timeworn institution dedicated to mental improvement subsidized by Oscorp in the wake of all these unfortunate government cutbacks." His regurgitation of the designated PR speech about Ravencroft felt like a slap in the face to Harry.

"You're experimenting with people in there!" Harry shouted.

"Progress has its stepping stones. Your father knew that." Harry winced at the mention of Norman Osborn. Sure, his father and he hadn't gotten along too well. They hadn't even really spoken during Norman's last few years. But surely he wouldn't have been happy with this turn of events.

Menken continued his gleeful speech. "Now, in light of your deceptive criminal actions, you've been—how do I put this gently?—fired. The fall is fast and steep, Harry." He waved tauntingly. "Bye-bye!"

Harry lunged at Menken but was quickly grabbed by two Oscorp security guards. They started dragging him out of the office.

"You're not going to bury me, too!" Harry shouted. "You hear me?! You can't bury me!"

Menken gestured for the security men to stop. As he approached Harry, he looked the young man up and down. Noticing a series of flaking scales on Harry's neck, Menken was reminded of how Norman Osborn looked during his last, bedridden days.

"Seems to me like you're halfway in the ground already. It's only a matter of time." He lowered his voice and looked Harry directly in the eyes. "You're going to die a painful death, just like your father. The difference is . . . no one is going to miss you."

Harry spat in Menken's face. Disgusted, Menken yelled, "Get him out of here!"

The security guards grabbed Harry's arms more firmly and hauled him out of the office.

Menken looked at Felicia, who was standing open-mouthed in the corner. He wiped the saliva off his face.

"You work for me now," he told her.

CHAPTER 8
BREAKING OUT

A SLEEK, SHINY SEDAN pulled up to the Ravencroft Institute like a black snake winding its way up a hill.

The guard at the gate dutifully approached the tinted window, his trusty clipboard in hand. "Can I help you?" he asked as the window rolled down to reveal a young man sitting tensely in the backseat.

"Yeah," the passenger replied, clearly agitated. "You can open the gate. I'm Harry Osborn. As in 'Oscorp.' The name on all the trucks over there, not to mention on *your* paycheck."

The guard quickly scanned his clipboard. "Uh . . .

Mr. Osborn . . . we don't have you on the list, sir. I'll have to call it in."

"I'm not on the list, Frank," Harry said tersely, glancing at the man's badge. "I *am* the list. Actually, I'll make a new list starting with Frank-the-gate-guard-formerly-employed-by-Oscorp."

Frank froze, unsure how to proceed. His strict training had been quite explicit about security protocols . . . and what would happen to employees who broke them. On the other hand, he needed this job. There was no way he was going to lose it by offending the CEO of his company.

"There's a patient in the isolation wing I need to see. And you're going to take me there personally," Harry continued.

Frank supposed there was no other option. Harry was adamant. And he couldn't get fired for helping the boss, right?

Moments later, Frank was leading Harry through the asylum. Harry scanned the interior of the facility, observing a few jump-suited employees wheeling aluminum pallets toward the maximum-security wing. Who knew what sort of sick experiments they were conducting.

Just before they passed through the doors to the wing, another guard stopped them.

"Joe, this is Mr. Osborn," Frank explained pointedly. "Of *Oscorp*."

The guard called Joe eyed Harry up and down. Then he spoke. "I'm sorry, sir. Without a yellow badge, I can't let anyone past this poi—"

"Get your supervisor on the phone," Harry interrupted. "Now."

As the guard turned to the phone hanging on the wall, Harry swiftly grabbed the Taser off his hip and zapped him. Joe fell to the floor.

Frank reached for his gun, but Harry tased his arm before he could get to it. With both guards down for the count, Harry snatched the yellow badge off Joe's uniform and quickly dragged him away. It was show time.

Soon, Harry emerged from a supply closet a new

man: Joe, the Ravencroft security guard, to be exact. He used his newly acquired yellow badge to swipe a reader; the doors to the isolation wing swung open, and Harry stalked through.

All the aluminum pallets he'd seen earlier were being dropped off in one particular procedure room. The coast was clear. He could guess which electrically charged patient that room housed. Suddenly, the thick doors to the room swung open.

". . . keep him sedated with four hundred mgs of sodium thiopental and phenobarbital. It'll hold him in an induced coma until we start phase two of testing."

Harry kept his face low until he was sure the doctor and med techs had passed. Then he watched the group disappear down the hallway.

With the hall clear, Harry walked up to the room's observation window. There he was: Electro. He was unconscious and confined by restraints. He looked bigger—and, strangely, brighter—in person.

Thinking fast, Harry pulled the fire alarm on the wall. *BEEP! BEEP! BEEP!* It screeched loudly.

Harry started to screech along with it. "This is an emergency evacuation! We have a gas leak! Everybody out now!"

Harry headed for Electro's room as employees flooded the corridor, again using his new yellow badge to enter the restricted area.

It was oddly still and quiet in the room. A stark difference from the chaos he had caused outside. He destroyed the main lock pad with the Taser, then approached the sleeping giant. Small tubes in his nose were connected to tanks on the ground. Harry turned the output valve, slowing the gas flow.

He had to get Electro to wake up *now*. Everyone would know there wasn't a real emergency any minute. And then they would come back here. Electro's eyes started to flutter open.

Good. He was coming out of it.

"Wake up," Harry said loudly.

Electro's eyes opened wider, looking at the strange young man in front of him. He felt disoriented and weakened. Feelings he *hated* experiencing.

"We don't have much time," Harry said. "I can get you out of here."

"Who . . . are you?" Electro asked groggily.

"Harry Osborn. I want to make you a deal."

Electro's eyes narrowed at the sound of the name. "Osssss . . . born? I should . . . kill you."

"Think bigger, Max." Harry made sure to use Electro's former name, hoping to spark an immediate kinship with him. He needed Electro to trust him. "I'm not the one you want. You want Spider-Man. I can give him to you."

Now Electro's eyes gleamed. Harry wasn't sure whether it was the name "Max" or "Spider-Man" that had piqued the guy's interest, but he knew he had to keep it.

"How?"

Dr. Kafka was not pleased. He'd been planning on taking a nice coffee break and typing up his latest research on his prime patient, Electro. He knew he was on the verge of a breakthrough with the crazy sparkler.

And then the fire alarm went off. And then there were talks of a gas leak, and then of a false alarm and a break-in. This was no way to work. He wanted answers. Now.

He marched into the Ravencroft security room.

"What's happening?" he demanded of the security tech.

"Someone pulled the alarm in the iso wing. . . ."

Alarmed, Kafka glanced up at the bank of closed-circuit monitors. A young man he didn't recognize was in Electro's room.

"Who the hell is that?" he asked, gesturing wildly at the screen.

The tech went pale. "I . . . I'm . . ." he stammered.

"Get a containment team up there. NOW!" Kafka shouted.

Back in Electro's room, Harry heard rapid movement outside. He knew he had to talk. Fast.

"You want to take all the power from the city, right?"

Electro glared at him. "You couldn't possibly know what I want."

"I know everything about you," Harry responded. "Electrical engineering. You submitted a design for the grid, and they *stole* it."

Electro shifted slightly, which Harry took as a sign to go on. "That's why you want it. To take back what's yours. All the power in the city. The power you deserve right at your fingertips. You'll never be invisible again, Max."

Harry leaned closer. "But I need something first. I need you to get me into Oscorp."

Electro blinked at him, confused. "What do you mean, 'get you in'? It's yours."

"Not anymore," Harry explained. "Oscorp betrayed us both. I can't get in there without you, and you can't get out of here without me. And then, once you shut down the grid, Spider-Man will come for you. . . . I want you to make him bleed."

"Why do you want him to bleed?" Electro asked.

"Let's just say I don't like taking no for an answer."

Suddenly, there was a loud noise from just outside the door. The Ravencroft guards were trying to get in through a combination of hot-wiring the broken lock pad and brute force.

Harry cranked his Taser up to the maximum energy level.

"Give me one reason why I should trust you," Electro challenged.

"Because I need you."

Those were the magic words. Electro had never been truly needed by anyone. It felt good. He needed to know it was true.

Harry looked him directly in the eyes. "I need you. You're the only one that can help save my life."

Electro couldn't get enough. "One more time."

"Please."

At that moment, the doors burst open, and guards

in black uniforms rushed inside, their weapons raised.

Before they reached him, Harry managed to zap Electro with the Taser. It hadn't reached full charge yet, but it was enough to get Electro going. The glowing villain could feel the now-familiar buzzing sensation of electricity circulating throughout his body.

The guards reached Harry and started dragging him away. Harry fought against them with all the strength he had.

"They're going to make you disappear!" Harry yelled hurriedly at Electro. "I know what it's like to be thrown away. Please, *Max! Help me!*"

The butt of a rifle slammed into Harry's side, and he dropped helplessly to the floor.

Electro watched as Harry coughed, then winced with pain. Harry looked pale and weak. A bolt of fury surged through Electro. Somebody finally needed him, and that somebody was being pulled away. No. He was not going to let them get away with this.

The energy particles within him started to build

dangerously, and the room's atmosphere noticeably changed. The guards stopped what they were doing, their hair spiking with static electricity.

A white blinding whirl of electricity flashed.

"Whoa," uttered a guard a second later.

Electro was gone.

Then, as if on some sort of sick cue, loud music started to blare from the intercom system. The lights flashed on and off to the beat. In another context, it might have been festive—a sign of a fun party about to get under way. To the guards, it was merely frightening.

Suddenly, a bolt of electricity shot out of a socket and zipped around the room, shattering the observation window. The guards put their hands up to avoid the flying glass, unsure what else to do. In an instant, the bolt whirled around them, knocking each one out with a small electric shock.

As soon as all the guards lay unconscious on the floor, the bolt started to spread out and form into a new shape. A shimmering, rejuvenated Electro appeared. His body longed to be rejoined with the currents running through the walls. He grinned at the discovery of a new facet of his power. He could take shape as electrical currents? He was unstoppable.

Electro stalked over to the man who had helped him reach his potential. The man who needed him. Harry looked up. He was still very much in pain.

"You wanna be my friend?" Electro asked him.

"I wanna be your friend," Harry responded, picking himself up gingerly.

"I had a friend once. Didn't work out."

Harry nodded knowingly. "Me, too."

Electro paused, looking at Harry for a long moment. Finally, he nodded back, sealing their sinister partnership.

"All right then," Electro said. "Let's go catch a spider."

CHAPTER 9

A CITY GOES BLACK

A MAN IN A BLACK SUIT rushed into Norman Osborn's penthouse office . . . now Donald Menken's office. The building's security had been compromised, and he needed to get Menken out.

"We have to move now!" he shouted at Menken.

Menken frowned and rose from behind the desk. "Why? What's happening?"

Suddenly, an electric bolt shot from the socket on the wall, knocking out the man in the black suit. Electro materialized in front of the desk.

"Remember me?"

Before Menken could even consider fleeing, Electro shot a rapid fire of bolts from his hands, shattering the glass desktop and flinging the steel sides of the desk to opposite walls. Menken backed away, cowering in the corner of the office. Suddenly, an all-too-familiar voice floated into the room.

"Oh, how the tables have turned."

Menken's eyes darted to the door, where he saw one Harry Osborn saunter in.

"I know it's hard to admit, but how spectacular is this move? Am I right?"

"Right as rain," Electro answered his new friend.

Harry rubbed his hands gleefully as he approached the cowering Menken. Revenge felt *good*. "Okay, Fairy Godmother, time to grant me a wish. I want in to Special Projects."

He'd formed this ingenious plan with his glowing comrade only moments ago. They were going to divide and conquer, with Harry exploring the secret Oscorp database and Electro fulfilling his ambition of taking over the power plant and placing the city in darkness while going after Spider-Man. Harry figured Special Projects would have all his father's research and then some. If the key to a cure existed anywhere, it would be there. And even if he couldn't find anything, he'd have Spider-Man at his disposal, thanks to Electro.

"Not a chance," Menken replied.

Harry made a buzzing sound. "*EH!* That's not the answer I was looking for!" He nodded at Electro, who moved toward the trembling man. Menken broke immediately, telling Harry exactly how to get into the top-secret Oscorp division.

Satisfied, Harry left Electro to do his thing, hearing the delightful sounds of electric buzzing and screaming. *Things are looking up,* he thought, a sinister smile spreading on his face. It felt good to have powerful friends.

Gwen couldn't believe it. The day had finally arrived. She was leaving for England in only a few hours. She sighed as she looked out the window of her cab. She was really going to miss the city. And a few of its special inhabitants.

If she made her flight, that is. She took a closer look outside the cab. They were stuck in bumper-to-bumper traffic. Gwen inhaled, ready to ask the driver to take a different route.

But just then the cabbie jumped, pointing out the windshield. "It's Spider-Man!"

Gwen leaned forward. It was Spider-Man, indeed. And he was swinging back and forth across the Brooklyn Bridge. People in other cars started to shout and point, as well. Spidey was spelling something in his web like a bright red-and-blue Charlotte.

I LOVE YOU

Gwen lit up, smiling broadly. "Stop the cab!"

"Lady, I'm not even moving," the driver responded.

"Oh, yeah!" She tossed him some money and leapt out of the car into traffic.

Spotting her from a distance, Spider-Man swooped down and grabbed her, bringing her up to a steel girder on the top of the bridge. The view was incredible, the sun setting over Manhattan.

"Hi," Spider-Man started.

"Hi," Gwen replied.

"I found you."

Gwen reached up and gently pulled off his mask. "I found you."

Peter smiled at her. "You got my message."

"That was you?" Gwen teased. "I didn't bring my glasses. What did it say?"

"It says 'I love you.' I do. I love you, Gwen Stacy. And no offense, but you're dead wrong," Peter responded.

"About what?"

"About us being on different paths. You *are* my path. You're the only thing in my life that makes sense. And there are a million good reasons why we shouldn't be together." He paused, brushing away a lock of hair that had fallen into her eyes. "But I'm tired of all of them. Everybody has to make a choice, right? I choose you. So here's what I propose: England. For both of us."

Gwen blinked at him in surprise. She hadn't thought this was where he was going. "What?"

"I'm just going to keep following you. But not

from the top of buildings anymore. I'm actually going with you. I mean, there's crime there, too, right? And less guns."

"Peter . . ." Gwen started.

"And they still haven't caught Jack the Ripper. Plus, the buildings are shorter, so . . ."

Gwen cut Peter off with a long-overdue kiss. Then she spoke. "I choose you, too." She laughed. This was crazy. But it was perfect. "I love you, Pe—"

Suddenly, the couple was interrupted. The gleaming lights of the city went out. All of them. It was as if a giant had pulled the city's plug, abruptly plunging everyone into darkness. It was a major blackout. And Peter had a sinking feeling it wasn't an accident.

In the heart of Midtown, the Empire State Building went black. Traffic lights stopped working, causing cars to crash into each other.

Down below, the subways stopped, pitching the passengers into blackness. Thousands of people were trapped. They started panicking, trying their cell phones. No one could get a signal.

At the airport, frantic pilots were trying to reach the control tower. But all they were getting was static. How the heck were they going to land? What was going on?

And in the ICU at the hospital, the backup generators hadn't started up. Patients were hooked up to machines that had powered down and wouldn't turn back on. Aunt May, among other nurses and doctors, gathered all the battery-operated machines she could to save her patients.

Peter and Gwen looked at the black city from their perch.

"Electro," Peter said.

"He must have cut off the power to the whole city," Gwen observed.

Peter's mind was racing. "There's gotta be some kind of backup."

"There's an emergency reset at the power plant," Gwen told him, thinking of the Oscorp energy plans she had seen. "That must be where he is. If he cuts the transmission lines to the city, they'll never get the power back up."

Peter braced himself to move, and then looked down at his wrists. "How do I stop him? I can't even get close. He keeps frying my web-shooters."

"What about grounding them?" Gwen suggested.

"Rubber, plastic. I've tried everything."

Gwen wracked her brain. "You try magnetizing them?"

"Except that!"

"Remember first-grade science? Mr. Hartwell's class?" Gwen asked. "Magnetize a nail with a battery. It holds an electric charge. If we charge up your web-shooters with enough voltage . . ."

"They'll repel his electricity," Peter finished, grinning. Boy, he loved this woman!

Moments later, Spider-Man and Gwen swung down to the chaotic streets, landing right beside a police officer and his car.

"There's no need for panic! Everyone, back into your vehicles and return to your homes. Let's all stay calm!" the cop shouted into his megaphone.

Suddenly, he noticed the pair beside him. "Spider-Man!" he shouted loudly, making Spidey and Gwen cringe when the feedback from the mic hit their eardrums.

"Sorry," the officer said, lowering the megaphone. "Glad to see ya."

"Huh? I'm deaf! Am I talking louder than normal right now?" Spidey shouted loudly.

Gwen stepped in. "Officer, my father was George Stacy, captain in the 19th precinct."

"Sure, I knew him. We all did. What can I do for ya?" the officer replied.

"We need your jumper cables."

In the control station of the Oscorp Power Plant, dozens of techs worked furiously to restore the city's power.

"Hit the emergency reset button!" yelled the station chief.

A nearby tech pulled a small key out from around his neck and ran to the emergency control box that housed the shiny red button. Just as he was about to fit the key into the lock, the observation windows burst. Glass shattered everywhere.

Electro charged inside the plant, shocking the man before he could hit the button. Turning to the station chief, Electro smiled. "Power to the people. I'll take it from here."

He shocked the chief and the rest of the techs before heading outside. Now it was time for some *real* fun. The Oscorp energy project had been his life when he was Max Dillon. He knew the plans for this plant backward and forward. And now it was time to take back what was rightfully his: the power. *All of it.*

Hovering over the gigantic towers, Electro smirked at the complex grid of thick cables that powered the city. Concentrating on his powers like a sorcerer, Electro dematerialized into a particle cloud and disappeared into the main cable. After a moment, all the lines glowed cherry red and swelled with energy.

Suddenly, the cables exploded. Massive amounts of electricity swirled and flew around. What was left of the cables dropped uselessly to the ground. As the electrical particles reformed into Electro, the villain noticed that a certain web-slinger had swung up to the perimeter wall.

Electro grinned. It looked like he and Harry would both be getting what they wanted tonight.

"You're too late," Electro told Spidey. "I cut the main line to the city. Now they'll know how it feels to live in the dark, crying out for help. But no one's coming to save them. Not even my old friend, 'Amazing.'"

"I see you're still crazy," Spider-Man observed.

"No, no, no. For the first time in my life, I'm sane. I understand now. You were in my life for a reason. So I could end yours."

Spider-Man took this in, locking eyes with Electro. "I get that. But I just need to know one thing." He paused dramatically. "Can you teach me the Electric Slide?"

Electro grinned with wicked rage. "With pleasure."

He fired electric bolts rapidly at Spider-Man, who quickly swung away. The blasts ripped the edge of the wall, fusing steel on a glowing track.

Spider-Man shot a web from his new location on the other side of the plant, snagging one of the hydraulic pumps. He used it like a hose, blasting water toward Electro. It had worked last time. Maybe it would be just as easy this time.

But as soon as the liquid reached Electro, the villain furrowed his brow in concentration. He stretched out his hands, instantly vaporizing the water into mist. His grin grew wider.

"You're gonna have to do better than that," he goaded Spider-Man, sending more bolts toward the hero. The bursts of electricity glowed brightly as they sailed through the air. They were more powerful and more controlled than ever before.

He's getting stronger, Spider-Man thought. He dodged the next bolt just in the nick of time. He'd felt the buzzing next to his side. That had been way too close.

"I'm really seeing the benefits of green energy right now," Spidey quipped tiredly.

Growing weary of all the bobbing and weaving, Spider-Man lunged at Electro full-force. They rolled on the ground, and Spidey kicked Electro hard, propelling him skyward. Then he shot up a web to lasso the glowing fiend.

Electro merely smiled, remembering how poorly Spidey's webs had reacted to his energy the last time. He sent more concentrated electric bursts down Spidey's web toward his web-shooters, expecting to hear them short out at any second. But the shooters simply hummed happily. As the charged bracelets perfectly repelled the bolt, Electro's eyes widened with surprise. They weren't supposed to do that!

Spidey clenched the lasso and yanked Electro hard back to the ground. The villain lay there, shaking.

With his foe momentarily dazed, Spidey quickly combed his brain for a new plan. He could almost hear Gwen's voice. *You got this, Peter. What else do you know about electricity?* And suddenly, an old memory sprung to mind: his computer shorting out after an electrical surge during one particular storm. He had an idea.

As Electro started to pick himself up, Spider-Man shot a web at the power-generator lever and pulled it up to the highest level. Electro charged toward Spider-Man, furious Spidey wasn't dead yet. Spidey grabbed two power cables and pressed the ends against Electro's body. Nothing would reboot the plant better than a Super Villain made out of electricity.

Just then, the power generator whirled to life. A tremendous burst of electricity coursed through the cable and into Electro. Spidey quickly jumped away to safety.

BOOM.

Electro seemed to burst with a blinding light. From afar, the scene might have looked like a fireworks display. And after a few seconds, it was over. Electro slumped to the ground, unconscious. He was no longer glowing. He had gotten exactly what he'd wanted—more power—and it'd taken all *his* powers away.

Spidey looked down at the defeated villain,

confident Electro would not be able to cause any more trouble. Thanks to Gwen, he'd saved the day once more. And though he was exhausted, dirty, and sore, it felt great. This was what being Spider-Man was all about. Helping people. Keeping the city safe.

Thinking once more of his leading lady, Spidey smiled. He pulled off his mask and took in the view— the New York City skyline at sunrise. It was beautiful. And yet he was excited to leave it behind.

Spider-Man put his mask back on and swung over the city. He was ready for the new challenges ahead. It was time for new amazing adventures.